There was once a man called Paikea who lived in faraway Hawaiki. One day, while swimming, he got into trouble and called for help. A young whale heard him and rescued him. As they grew up, Paikea and his whale became like brothers; and that whale brought Paikea to Aotearoa, New Zealand — to Whangara.

When he landed here he had magic spears that he threw into the air. Some became birds. Others became blossoming trees, fruits and flowers. Even more became fishes of the sea. But there was one magic spear, so it is said, that refused to leave his hands. So Paikea said a prayer over it: 'Go, fly forward into the future and flower when you are needed most.'

Many, many years later, Kahu was born to Porourangi, the eldest son of the whanau. When Koro Apirana, her grandfather, was told, he was disgusted.

'A girl,' he said. 'I will have nothing to do with her. She has broken the male line of descent from Paikea, our original ancestor.'

Somewhere in the sky the last magic spear that Paikea had thrown began its downward journey.

At the time, Kahu's mother, Rehua, had died giving birth to her. Her father, Porourangi, couldn't stop grieving for his wife so he went overseas and left Kahu to be brought up by the family: her grandfather Koro Apirana; her grandmother Nani Flowers; her Uncle Rawiri; and all who live in our village of Whangara.

During all the time she was growing up, Kahu tried to show Koro Apirana that even though she was a girl she was just as good as any boy. But still he would have nothing to do with her.

Nani Flowers scolded him, saying, 'Haven't you heard, you old paka? Girls can do anything these days.'
'That may be so,' Koro Apirana replied. 'But that doesn't mean they have the right.'
'Why doesn't my paka want me?' Kahu asked Nani Flowers.

Nani Flowers pointed to the gable on our meeting house: a carving of a man riding on a whale. And she told Kahu the story of Paikea. 'Ever since,' she continued, 'all the first-born have been sons. Then you were born.'

Just as Nani Flowers was speaking, a hole opened in the sky and something flashed out of it. It looked like a magic spear.

Part Two

That summer Whangara was beset with many troubles. The drought that had first begun some eight years ago reached its climax in hot days when the sun scorched the earth. The fishing grounds that once teemed with fish were now empty. People were having to leave the village to find work.

Concerned, Koro Apirana began to look for the answer. Why?

He blamed Kahu. 'When she was born,' he said, 'that's when things started to go wrong for us. She has broken the line back to the ancient ones. We have to put things right again. I want all the first-born boys of the area, those who were born when Kahu was, to be brought here to Whangara to undergo tests of strength and wisdom. One of them will be the leader we are looking for.'

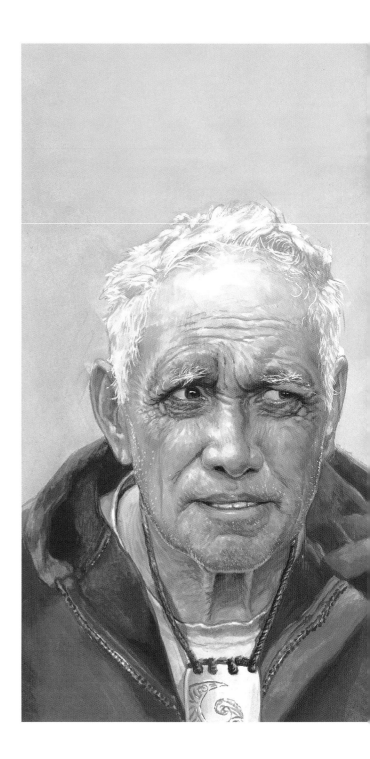

So began the Schools of Learning. The boys arrived by bus every weekend and underwent instructions in the arts designed to sharpen the skills of the intellect, body and spirit. From the very beginning Kahu rebelled at being left out — and Nani Flowers was at her side.

When the boys arrived on the first day she instructed Kahu to lead them on to the marae. Once the welcomes were over Kahu took her seat among the boys, but after that she was not allowed in.

She would try to listen in at the doorway to the meeting house or under the eaves of the windows and Koro Apirana knew she was there but could never catch her. Watching her, Nani Flowers, playing cards with her old friends Maka and Mere, would nod approvingly. 'You stay, Kahu,' she would say under her breath. 'You show the old paka.'

Kahu would watch from the flax bushes as the boys practised with warrior weapons. 'This is sacred work,' Koro Apirana would yell. 'And I will not let you jeopardise it.' But Kahu was stubborn. She asked Uncle Rawiri to teach her some moves with the fighting staffs. She became very skilled at it.

One of the boys, Hemi, was boastful and discovered her practising with her fighting staff and challenged her to a duel. He thought he would win. But Kahu beat him.

At that moment Koro Apirana walked around the corner and caught her. 'You have broken the sacredness of this School of Learning,' he said.

As if to confirm his words, that day a large school of more than 200 small pilot whales stranded themselves on a beach not far from Whangara. Helicopters dropped whale rescuers into the sea. Men and women from surrounding beach houses — even the old people from the local rest home — came to help. Despite all the efforts of the local community the whales could not be turned back to the sea.

'Did I cause this?' Kahu wondered, horrified.

Then, it was time for the last of the tests — the main test that would reveal which boy would become the next male successor in the village. Koro Apirana took them out on to the sea. He had a pendant around his neck, a whalebone tooth, worn by all the chiefs of Whangara. He threw it into the water.

'One of you must bring it back,' he said. 'Whoever it is will be the boy to lead us.'

The boys dived into the water. One by one they ran out of breath. One of them, Ropata, managed to grasp it but Hemi fought him underwater and the whalebone tooth fell back into the reef where it was very dark.

All the boys failed.

When he returned home that evening Koro Apirana was bereft. 'Do you realise what you've done?' he asked Kahu.

Kahu tried to make amends. She asked Uncle Rawiri to take her out on to the sea. When they arrived at the place where Koro Apirana had thrown the whalebone tooth she said, 'You wait here, Uncle Rawiri. I won't be long.'

She dived deep, deep, deep. She saw the whalebone tooth pendant and with her last bit of breath she reached out and grasped it.

'Here, you can give paka his pendant when we get home,' she told Uncle Rawiri when she surfaced. 'And I got us a crayfish for tea.'

But instead of giving the pendant to Koro Apirana, Uncle Rawiri gave it to Nani Flowers. 'Don't tell the old paka,' she said. 'He's not ready yet.' All along Nani Flowers had known Kahu was supposed to be the leader.

A few nights later Kahu's school had their break-up concert. She had a secret present for her Koro — she had won the local speech competition with a speech she had written about him. But Paka didn't turn up. Kahu gave her speech to an empty chair. 'This speech is a token of my great love and respect for my grandfather, ...' she began.

Back at home Nani Flowers tried to console her.

'It's not Paka's fault that I'm a girl,' Kahu said sadly. She began to weep and, just as her ancient ancestor, Paikea, had done, she called for help.

And far away, the whales heard her.

Part Three

Far away, on the other side of the sea, the whales were on their annual trek from the whale crib near South America, where young whales are born. They were an old herd, some sixty strong, led by an ancient battle-scarred bull whale. He had a moko on his head and he was the oldest whale in the sea; he looked a little like Koro Apirana. Wherever he went he was looked after by the old mother whale and her ladies in waiting — they looked like Nani Flowers and her card-playing friends, Maka and Mere. The tribe of whales followed along behind their leader, male, female and baby whales. Protecting them were warrior whales, watching from the front and sides and protecting the tribe from the rear as it made its pilgrimage through the hostile sea.

At Easter Island the whales were attacked by sharks. When the tribe neared French Polynesia, the ancient leader was hunted by whalers. He rammed one of the boats, its propellers threatening to shred him, as he shepherded his tribe to safety by way of a deep underground channel in the ocean floor. Man, who had once been the whales' brother, was now the most hostile enemy of all.

The ancient bull whale led the tribe to its Antarctic sanctuary where he hoped they would be safe from danger.

Then he heard Kahu calling to him. In his memory he thought it was the voice of his beloved rider, Paikea. When Paikea called he always obeyed. Immediately he set course through the Antarctic ice floes for Whangara.

It was a stormy day when the ancient bull whale and his herd reached Whangara. The waves were crashing on the beach.

As soon as Koro Apirana saw the whale tribe coming through the waves, he knew that Whangara was about to face its most crucial test. The ancient bull whale heaved himself on to the sand, stranding himself high above the high-water mark. Koro Apirana knew that the survival of Whangara depended on the survival of the whale.

'Once the world was a place where man, beasts and gods lived closely with one another,' he told the villagers that night. 'Then man became arrogant and set himself above all others. He divided his world into that half he could believe in and that half he could not believe in. He divided the world between the real and the unreal, the natural and the supernatural, the scientific and the fantastic, the present and the past. But the ancient whale has come back to remind us of the oneness we once had. If we are able to turn the whale back to sea, we honour that oneness — the whale will live and we will live. If we can't, the oneness has gone — the whale will die and all that we believe in will die.'

The village sprang into action. The men brought ropes and tied them around the whale's body, hoping to float him at high tide. Uncle Rawiri led the men, ordering a tractor to come to help with the pulling on the ropes. He dived under the whale to secure the rope around its body.

When high tide came, the men began a chant and tried to turn the whale. Nani Flowers, watching from the meeting house, gave a cry of dismay when the rope suddenly snapped.

She turned to the women: 'Come on,' she ordered.

But it was no use. The whale would not be moved.

Nobody saw Kahu as she slipped into the sea. Nobody realised she was gone as she climbed on top of the whale and settled herself in position.

'This is all my fault,' she said. All she knew was that she loved her Paka and her tribe and that she was the only one who could save them. 'Goodbye, Paka,' she called. 'Goodbye, Nani. Goodbye, Whangara. Live for ever.' She was not afraid to die.

She kicked at the whale as if it were a horse. 'Come on, let's go,' she commanded. 'Return to the sea.'

Uncle Rawiri turned for one last look at the whales and saw Kahu.

But it was too late. Kahu was already leaving with the whales.

Suddenly the moon came out. Kahu felt a shiver run through the ancient whale and knew it was going to dive. She placed her head against its breathing hole and, wonder of wonders, when the whale dived she was surrounded with bubbles of air. The first dive was shallow and when the whale surfaced she took a deep breath.

The whale dived deeper and, this time, Kahu felt her arms and legs clamped tight by the ancient bull whale's muscles. So this was how Paikea was able to ride the whale without falling off! Again she was able to breathe through the whale's spout.

Then came the third dive and Kahu knew that this time would be for ever. All around her whales were sounding, sounding, sounding. 'I am not afraid to die,' Kahu said.

The whale's body arched and slid into a deep dive. The huge flukes stroked at the rain-drenched surface. Slowly, one by one, the whale tribe slid beneath the sea.

No,' Nani Flowers cried. She ran into the waves and some of the men had to run in after her. She could only watch, her heart breaking, as Kahu disappeared. She turned to Koro Apirana and handed him his whale-tooth pendant.

'Which of the boys?' he asked. 'Which of the boys?'

Nani Flowers pointed to the sea. Only then did he understand that the reason why things had been going wrong was not because Kahu was a girl but because he had been trying to deny her birthright.

Part Four

In the sunless sea, sixty whales were sounding slowly, steeply diving. An ancient bull whale, bearing a sacred sign, was in the middle of the herd. Flanking him were the old mother whale, her ladies in waiting and the rest of the whale tribe. Wherever the tribe went, the sea honoured the ancient bull whale, the koroua, for he was legendary and much loved.

Her royal husband might be legendary but suddenly the old mother whale realised what was happening. She remembered her husband's story of Paikea and his last magic spear, the spear that wouldn't leave his hand. She knew he thought he was still carrying Paikea on his back — and she also knew that this was not Paikea but a human child.

Husband, stop,' she called. 'The human on your back isn't Paikea. It is the last spear. It is the magic spear. This is the spear that was to go into the future, the one to flower when it was needed most.'

The old bull whale weighed her words and the weight of the rider on his back and he knew the old mother whale was right.

'We must return to Whangara,' he commanded.

Slowly the phalanx of whales began their graceful procession to the surface of the sea.

And Kahu gave a huge gasp.

Kahu looked around the hospital room — Koro Apirana and Nani Flowers were beside her bed and waiting behind them were Uncle Rawiri, Maka and Mere and others from Whangara.

'I fell off the whale,' Kahu said. 'If I were a boy I would have held on tight. I'm sorry, Paka, I'm not a boy.'

'Boy or girl, it doesn't matter,' Koro Apirana answered. 'I acknowledge you, granddaughter. Take your rightful place.'

From the backwash of time came the voice of the old mother whale: 'Child, your people await you. Return to the Kingdom of Man and fulfil your destiny.'

The sea was drenched with glorious echoing whalesong, filled with magnificence, love — and hope.

About the Author

Witi Ihimaera is a pioneer in world indigenous literature. His debut work, *Pounamu Pounamu* (1972), was the first collection of short stories by a Maori, while *Tangi* (1973) was the first novel by a Maori. A prolific writer and editor who also had a distinguished career as a diplomat, his works include ten novels, five short-story collections, five opera and orchestral works, and numerous anthologies and non-fiction works. He is now a professor of English at the University of Auckland. *The Whale Rider* is Witi's best-known work, and was made into an internationally acclaimed movie directed by Niki Caro. The novel has been translated into numerous languages and has won readers around the world.

About the Illustrator

Bruce Potter began his art career as a cartoonist and caricaturist for a number of different newspapers around the world. He has been self-employed as a portrait painter specialising in oils, and he started illustrating children's books about four years ago. Bruce lives on two acres of land in Tuakau, south of Auckland, with his wife and three children, all of whom have appeared in his books at one time or another.